melville house classics

MAY DAY

MAY DAY

F. SCOTT FITZGERALD

MELVILLE HOUSE PUBLISHING
BROOKLYN, NEW YORK

MAY DAY WAS FIRST PUBLISHED IN 1920 (SMART SET COMPANY, INC.).

SERIES DESIGN: DAVID KONOPKA

MELVILLE HOUSE PUBLISHING
145 PLYMOUTH STREET
BROOKLYN, NY 11201

WWW.MHPBOOKS.COM

ISBN: 978-1-933633-43-5

FIRST MELVILLE HOUSE PRINTING: MAY 2009

LIBRARY OF CONGRESS CATALOGING-IN-PUBLICATION DATA

FITZGERALD, F. SCOTT (FRANCIS SCOTT), 1896-1940.
  MAY DAY / F. SCOTT FITZGERALD.
    P. CM.
  ISBN 978-1-933633-43-5
  I. TITLE.
  PS3511.I9M39 2008
  813'.52--DC22
                              2008009211

MAY DAY

There had been a war fought and won and the great city of the conquering people was crossed with triumphal arches and vivid with thrown flowers of white, red, and rose. All through the long spring days the returning soldiers marched up the chief highway behind the strump of drums and the joyous, resonant wind of the brasses, while merchants and clerks left their bickerings and figurings and, crowding to the windows, turned their white-bunched faces gravely upon the passing battalions.

Never had there been such splendor in the great city, for the victorious war had brought plenty in its train, and the merchants had flocked thither from the South and West with their households to taste of all the luscious feasts and witness the lavish entertainments prepared—and to buy for their women furs against the next winter and bags of golden mesh and varicolored slippers of silk and silver and rose satin and cloth of gold.

So gaily and noisily were the peace and prosperity impending hymned by the scribes and poets of the conquering people that more and more spenders had gathered from the provinces to drink the wine of excitement, and faster and faster did the merchants dispose of their trinkets and slippers until they sent up a mighty cry for more trinkets and more slippers in order that they might give in barter what was demanded of them. Some even of them flung up their hands helplessly, shouting:

"Alas! I have no more slippers! and alas! I have no more trinkets! May Heaven help me, for I know not what I shall do!"

But no one listened to their great outcry, for the throngs were far too busy—day by day, the foot-soldiers trod jauntily the highway and all exulted because the young men returning were pure and brave, sound of tooth and pink of cheek, and the young women of the land were virgins and comely both of face and of figure.

So during all this time there were many adventures that happened in the great city, and, of these, several—or perhaps one—are here set down.

I   At nine o'clock on the morning of the first of May, 1919, a young man spoke to the room clerk at the Biltmore Hotel, asking if Mr. Philip Dean were registered there, and if so, could he be connected with Mr. Dean's rooms. The inquirer was dressed in a well-cut, shabby suit. He was small, slender, and darkly handsome; his eyes were framed above with unusually long eyelashes and below with the blue semicircle of ill health, this latter effect heightened by an unnatural glow which colored his face like a low, incessant fever.

Mr. Dean was staying there. The young man was directed to a telephone at the side.

After a second his connection was made; a sleepy voice hello'd from somewhere above.

"Mr. Dean?"—this very eagerly—"it's Gordon, Phil. It's Gordon Sterrett. I'm downstairs. I heard you were in New York and I had a hunch you'd be here."

The sleepy voice became gradually enthusiastic. Well, how was Gordy, old boy! Well, he certainly was surprised and tickled! Would Gordy come right up, for Pete's sake!

A few minutes later Philip Dean, dressed in blue silk pajamas, opened his door and the two young men greeted each other with a half-embarrassed exuberance. They were both about twenty-four, Yale graduates of the year before the war; but there the resemblance stopped abruptly. Dean was blond, ruddy, and rugged under his thin pajamas. Everything about him radiated fitness and bodily comfort. He smiled frequently, showing large and prominent teeth.

"I was going to look you up," he cried enthusiastically. "I'm taking a couple of weeks off. If you'll sit down a sec I'll be right with you. Going to take a shower."

As he vanished into the bathroom his visitor's dark eyes roved nervously around the room, resting for a moment on a great English travelling bag in the corner and on a family of thick silk shirts littered on the chairs amid impressive neckties and soft woollen socks.

Gordon rose and, picking up one of the shirts, gave it a minute examination. It was of very heavy silk, yellow, with a pale blue stripe—and there were nearly a dozen of them. He stared involuntarily at his own shirt-cuffs—they were ragged and linty at the edges and soiled to a faint gray. Dropping the silk shirt, he held his coat-sleeves down and worked the frayed shirt-cuffs up till they were out of sight. Then he went to the mirror and looked at himself with listless, unhappy interest. His tie, of former glory, was faded and thumb-creased—it served no longer to hide the jagged buttonholes of his collar. He thought, quite without amusement, that only three years before he had received a scattering vote in the senior elections at college for being the best-dressed man in his class.

Dean emerged from the bathroom polishing his body.

"Saw an old friend of yours last night," he remarked. "Passed her in the lobby and couldn't think of her name to save my neck. That girl you brought up to New Haven senior year."

Gordon started.

"Edith Bradin? That whom you mean?"

"'At's the one. Damn good looking. She's still sort of a pretty doll—you know what I mean: as if you touched her she'd smear."

He surveyed his shining self complacently in the mirror, smiled faintly, exposing a section of teeth.

"She must be twenty-three anyway," he continued.

"Twenty-two last month," said Gordon absently.

"What? Oh, last month. Well, I imagine she's down for the Gamma Psi dance. Did you know we're having a Yale Gamma Psi dance tonight at Delmonico's? You better come up, Gordy. Half of New Haven'll probably be there. I can get you an invitation."

Draping himself reluctantly in fresh underwear, Dean lit a cigarette and sat down by the open window, inspecting his calves and knees under the morning sunshine which poured into the room.

"Sit down, Gordy," he suggested, "and tell me all about what you've been doing and what you're doing now and everything."

Gordon collapsed unexpectedly upon the bed; lay there inert and spiritless. His mouth, which habitually dropped a little open when his face was in repose, became suddenly helpless and pathetic.

"What's the matter?" asked Dean quickly.

"Oh, God!"

"What's the matter?"

"Every God damn thing in the world," he said miserably. "I've absolutely gone to pieces, Phil. I'm all in."

"Huh?"

"I'm all in." His voice was shaking.

Dean scrutinized him more closely with appraising blue eyes.

"You certainly look all shot."

"I am. I've made a hell of a mess of everything." He paused. "I'd better start at the beginning—or will it bore you?"

"Not at all; go on." There was, however, a hesitant note in Dean's voice. This trip East had been planned for a holiday—to find Gordon Sterrett in trouble exasperated him a little.

"Go on," he repeated, and then added half under his breath, "Get it over with."

"Well," began Gordon unsteadily, "I got back from France in February, went home to Harrisburg for a month, and then came down to New York to get a job. I got one—with an export company. They fired me yesterday."

"Fired you?"

"I'm coming to that, Phil. I want to tell you frankly. You're about the only man I can turn to in a matter like this. You won't mind if I just tell you frankly, will you, Phil?"

Dean stiffened a bit more. The pats he was bestowing on his knees grew perfunctory. He felt vaguely that he was being unfairly saddled with responsibility; he was not even sure he wanted to be told. Though never surprised at finding Gordon Sterrett in mild difficulty, there was something in this present misery that repelled him and hardened him, even though it excited his curiosity.

"Go on."

"It's a girl."

"Hm." Dean resolved that nothing was going to spoil his trip. If Gordon was going to be depressing, then he'd have to see less of Gordon.

"Her name is Jewel Hudson," went on the distressed voice from the bed. "She used to be 'pure,'

I guess, up to about a year ago. Lived here in New York—poor family. Her people are dead now and she lives with an old aunt. You see it was just about the time I met her that everybody began to come back from France in droves—and all I did was to welcome the newly arrived and go on parties with 'em. That's the way it started, Phil, just from being glad to see everybody and having them glad to see me."

"You ought to've had more sense."

"I know," Gordon paused, and then continued listlessly. "I'm on my own now, you know, and Phil, I can't stand being poor. Then came this darn girl. She sort of fell in love with me for a while and, though I never intended to get so involved, I'd always seem to run into her somewhere. You can imagine the sort of work I was doing for those exporting people—of course, I always intended to draw; do illustrating for magazines; there's a pile of money in it."

"Why didn't you? You've got to buckle down if you want to make good," suggested Dean with cold formalism.

"I tried, a little, but my stuff's crude. I've got talent, Phil; I can draw—but I just don't know how. I ought to go to art school and I can't afford it. Well, things came to a crisis about a week ago. Just as I was down to about my last dollar this girl began bothering me. She wants some money; claims she can make trouble for me if she doesn't get it."

"Can she?"

"I'm afraid she can. That's one reason I lost my

job—she kept calling up the office all the time, and that was sort of the last straw down there. She's got a letter all written to send to my family. Oh, she's got me, all right. I've got to have some money for her."

There was an awkward pause. Gordon lay very still, his hands clenched by his side.

"I'm all in," he continued, his voice trembling. "I'm half crazy, Phil. If I hadn't known you were coming East, I think I'd have killed myself. I want you to lend me three hundred dollars."

Dean's hands, which had been patting his bare ankles, were suddenly quiet—and the curious uncertainty playing between the two became taut and strained.

After a second Gordon continued:

"I've bled the family until I'm ashamed to ask for another nickel."

Still Dean made no answer.

"Jewel says she's got to have two hundred dollars."

"Tell her where she can go."

"Yes, that sounds easy, but she's got a couple of drunken letters I wrote her. Unfortunately she's not at all the flabby sort of person you'd expect."

Dean made an expression of distaste. "I can't stand that sort of woman. You ought to have kept away."

"I know," admitted Gordon wearily.

"You've got to look at things as they are. If you haven't got money you've got to work and stay away from women."

"That's easy for you to say," began Gordon, his eyes narrowing. "You've got all the money in the world."

"I most certainly have not. My family keep darn close tab on what I spend. Just because I have a little leeway I have to be extra careful not to abuse it."

He raised the blind and let in a further flood of sunshine.

"I'm no prig, Lord knows," he went on deliberately. "I like pleasure—and I like a lot of it on a vacation like this, but you're—you're in awful shape. I never heard you talk just this way before. You seem to be sort of bankrupt—morally as well as financially."

"Don't they usually go together?"

Dean shook his head impatiently.

"There's a regular aura about you that I don't understand. It's a sort of evil."

"It's an air of worry and poverty and sleepless nights," said Gordon, rather defiantly.

"I don't know."

"Oh, I admit I'm depressing. I depress myself. But, my God, Phil, a week's rest and a new suit and some ready money and I'd be like—like I was. Phil, I can draw like a streak, and you know it. But half the time I haven't had the money to buy decent drawing materials—and I can't draw when I'm tired and discouraged and all in. With a little ready money I can take a few weeks off and get started."

"How do I know you wouldn't use it on some other woman?"

"Why rub it in?" said Gordon quietly.

"I'm not rubbing it in. I hate to see you this way."

"Will you lend me the money, Phil?"

"I can't decide right off. That's a lot of money and it'll be darn inconvenient for me."

"It'll be hell for me if you can't—I know I'm whining, and it's all my own fault but—that doesn't change it."

"When could you pay it back?"

This was encouraging. Gordon considered. It was probably wisest to be frank.

"Of course, I could promise to send it back next month, but—I'd better say three months. Just as soon as I start to sell drawings."

"How do I know you'll sell any drawings?"

A new hardness in Dean's voice sent a faint chill of doubt over Gordon. Was it possible that he wouldn't get the money?

"I supposed you had a little confidence in me."

"I did have—but when I see you like this I begin to wonder."

"Do you suppose if I wasn't at the end of my rope I'd come to you like this? Do you think I'm enjoying it?" He broke off and bit his lip, feeling that he had better subdue the rising anger in his voice. After all, he was the suppliant.

"You seem to manage it pretty easily," said Dean angrily. "You put me in the position where, if I don't lend it to you, I'm a sucker—oh, yes, you do. And let me tell you it's no easy thing for me to get hold of three hundred dollars. My income isn't so big but that a slice like that won't play the deuce with it."

He left his chair and began to dress, choosing his clothes carefully. Gordon stretched out his arms and clenched the edges of the bed, fighting back a desire to cry out. His head was splitting and whirring, his mouth was dry and bitter and he could feel the fever in his blood resolving itself into innumerable regular counts like a slow dripping from a roof.

Dean tied his tie precisely, brushed his eyebrows, and removed a piece of tobacco from his teeth with solemnity. Next he filled his cigarette case, tossed the empty box thoughtfully into the wastebasket, and settled the case in his vest pocket.

"Had breakfast?" he demanded.

"No; I don't eat it any more."

"Well, we'll go out and have some. We'll decide about that money later. I'm sick of the subject. I came East to have a good time.

"Let's go over to the Yale Club," he continued moodily, and then added with an implied reproof: "You've given up your job. You've got nothing else to do."

"I'd have a lot to do if I had a little money," said Gordon pointedly.

"Oh, for Heaven's sake drop the subject for a while! No point in glooming on my whole trip. Here, here's some money."

He took a five-dollar bill from his wallet and tossed it over to Gordon, who folded it carefully and put it in his pocket. There was an added spot of color in his cheeks, an added glow that was not fever. For an instant before they turned to go out their eyes met and in that instant each found something that made him lower his own glance quickly. For in that instant they quite suddenly and definitely hated each other.

Fifth Avenue and Forty-fourth Street swarmed with the noon crowd. The wealthy, happy sun glittered in transient gold through the thick windows of the smart shops, lighting upon mesh bags and purses and strings of pearls in gray velvet cases; upon gaudy feather fans of many colors; upon the laces and silks of expensive dresses; upon the bad paintings and the fine period furniture in the elaborate show rooms of interior decorators.

Working-girls, in pairs and groups and swarms, loitered by these windows, choosing their future boudoirs from some resplendent display which included even a man's silk pajamas laid domestically across the bed. They stood in front of the jewelry stores and picked out their engagement rings, and their wedding rings and their platinum wristwatches, and then drifted on to inspect the feather fans and opera cloaks; meanwhile digesting the sandwiches and sundaes they had eaten for lunch.

All through the crowd were men in uniform, sailors from the great fleet anchored in the Hudson, soldiers with divisional insignia from Massachusetts to California, wanting fearfully to be noticed, and finding the great city thoroughly fed up with soldiers unless they were nicely massed into pretty formations and uncomfortable under the weight of a pack and rifle.

Through this medley Dean and Gordon wandered; the former interested, made alert by the display of humanity at its frothiest and gaudiest; the latter reminded of how often he had been one of the crowd, tired, casually fed, overworked, and dissipated. To Dean the struggle was significant, young, cheerful; to Gordon it was dismal, meaningless, endless.

In the Yale Club they met a group of their former classmates who greeted the visiting Dean vociferously. Sitting in a semicircle of lounges and great chairs, they had a highball all around.

Gordon found the conversation tiresome and interminable. They lunched together en masse, warmed with liquor as the afternoon began. They were all going to the Gamma Psi dance that night—it promised to be the best party since the war.

"Edith Bradin's coming," said someone to Gordon. "Didn't she used to be an old flame of yours? Aren't you both from Harrisburg?"

"Yes." He tried to change the subject. "I see her brother occasionally. He's sort of a socialistic nut. Runs a paper or something here in New York."

"Not like his gay sister, eh?" continued his eager informant. "Well, she's coming tonight with a junior named Peter Himmel."

Gordon was to meet Jewel Hudson at eight o'clock—he had promised to have some money for her. Several times he glanced nervously at his wristwatch. At four, to his relief, Dean rose and announced that he was going over to Rivers Brothers to buy some collars and ties. But as they left the Club another of the party joined them, to Gordon's great dismay. Dean was in a jovial mood now, happy, expectant of the evening's party, faintly hilarious. Over in Rivers' he chose a dozen neckties, selecting each one after long consultations with the other man. Did he think narrow ties were coming back? And wasn't it a shame that Rivers couldn't get any more Welsh Margotson collars? There never was a collar like the "Covington."

Gordon was in something of a panic. He wanted the money immediately. And he was now inspired also with a vague idea of attending the Gamma Psi dance. He wanted to see Edith—Edith whom he hadn't met since one romantic night at the Harrisburg Country Club just before he went to France. The affair had died, drowned in the turmoil of the war and quite forgotten in the arabesque of these three months, but a picture of her, poignant, debonnaire, immersed in her own inconsequential chatter, recurred to him unexpectedly and brought a hundred memories with it. It was Edith's face that he had cherished through college with a sort of detached yet affectionate admiration. He had loved to draw her—around his room had been a dozen sketches of her—playing golf, swimming—he could draw her pert, arresting profile with his eyes shut.

They left Rivers' at five-thirty and paused for a moment on the sidewalk.

"Well," said Dean genially, "I'm all set now. Think I'll go back to the hotel and get a shave, haircut, and massage."

"Good enough," said the other man, "I think I'll join you."

Gordon wondered if he was to be beaten after all. With difficulty he restrained himself from turning to the man and snarling out, "Go on away, damn you!" In despair he suspected that perhaps Dean had spoken to him, was keeping him along in order to avoid a dispute about the money.

They went into the Biltmore—a Biltmore alive with girls—mostly from the West and South, the stellar debutantes of many cities gathered for the dance of a famous fraternity of a famous university. But to Gordon they were faces in a dream. He gathered together his forces for a last appeal, was about to come out with he knew not what, when Dean suddenly excused himself to the other man and taking Gordon's arm led him aside.

"Gordy," he said quickly, "I've thought the whole thing over carefully and I've decided that I can't lend you that money. I'd like to oblige you, but I don't feel I ought to—it'd put a crimp in me for a month."

Gordon, watching him dully, wondered why he had never before noticed how much those upper teeth projected.

"—I'm mighty sorry, Gordon," continued Dean, "but that's the way it is."

He took out his wallet and deliberately counted out seventy-five dollars in bills.

"Here," he said, holding them out, "here's seventy-five; that makes eighty all together. That's all the actual cash I have with me, besides what I'll actually spend on the trip."

Gordon raised his clenched hand automatically, opened it as though it were tongs he was holding, and clenched it again on the money.

"I'll see you at the dance," continued Dean. "I've got to get along to the barber shop."

"So long," said Gordon in a strained and husky voice.

"So long."

Dean began to smile, but seemed to change his mind. He nodded briskly and disappeared.

But Gordon stood there, his handsome face awry with distress, the roll of bills clenched tightly in his hand. Then, blinded by sudden tears, he stumbled clumsily down the Biltmore steps.

III   About nine o'clock of the same night two human beings came out of a cheap restaurant in Sixth Avenue. They were ugly, ill-nourished, devoid of all except the very lowest form of intelligence, and without even that animal exuberance that in itself brings color into life; they were lately vermin-ridden, cold, and hungry in a dirty town of a strange land; they were poor, friendless; tossed as driftwood from their births, they would be tossed as driftwood to their deaths. They were dressed in the uniform of the United States Army, and on the shoulder of each was the insignia of a drafted division from New Jersey, landed three days before.

The taller of the two was named Carrol Key, a name hinting that in his veins, however thinly diluted by generations of degeneration, ran blood of some potentiality. But one could stare endlessly at the long, chinless face, the dull, watery eyes, and high cheekbones, without finding a suggestion of either ancestral worth or native resourcefulness.

His companion was swart and bandy-legged, with rat-eyes and a much-broken hooked nose. His defiant air was obviously a pretense, a weapon of protection borrowed from that world of snarl and snap, of physical bluff and physical menace, in which he had always lived. His name was Gus Rose.

Leaving the cafe they sauntered down Sixth Avenue, wielding toothpicks with great gusto and complete detachment.

"Where to?" asked Rose, in a tone which implied that he would not be surprised if Key suggested the South Sea Islands.

"What you say we see if we can getta holda some liquor?" Prohibition was not yet. The ginger in the suggestion was caused by the law forbidding the selling of liquor to soldiers.

Rose agreed enthusiastically.

"I got an idea," continued Key, after a moment's thought, "I got a brother somewhere."

"In New York?"

"Yeah. He's an old fella." He meant that he was an elder brother. "He's a waiter in a hash joint."

"Maybe he can get us some."

"I'll say he can!"

"B'lieve me, I'm goin' to get this darn uniform

off me tomorra. Never get me in it again, neither. I'm goin' to get me some regular clothes."

"Say, maybe I'm not."

As their combined finances were something less than five dollars, this intention can be taken largely as a pleasant game of words, harmless and consoling. It seemed to please both of them, however, for they reinforced it with chuckling and mention of personages high in biblical circles, adding such further emphasis as "Oh, boy!" "You know!" and "I'll say so!" repeated many times over.

The entire mental pabulum of these two men consisted of an offended nasal comment extended through the years upon the institution—army, business, or poorhouse—which kept them alive, and toward their immediate superior in that institution. Until that very morning the institution had been the "government" and the immediate superior had been the "Cap'n"—from these two they had glided out and were now in the vaguely uncomfortable state before they should adopt their next bondage. They were uncertain, resentful, and somewhat ill at ease. This they hid by pretending an elaborate relief at being out of the army, and by assuring each other that military discipline should never again rule their stubborn, liberty-loving wills. Yet, as a matter of fact, they would have felt more at home in a prison than in this new-found and unquestionable freedom.

Suddenly Key increased his gait. Rose, looking up and following his glance, discovered a crowd that was collecting fifty yards down the street. Key chuckled and began to run in the direction of the crowd; Rose thereupon also chuckled and his short bandy legs twinkled beside the long, awkward strides of his companion.

Reaching the outskirts of the crowd they immediately became an indistinguishable part of it. It was composed of ragged civilians somewhat the worse for liquor, and of soldiers representing many divisions and many stages of sobriety, all clustered around a gesticulating little Jew with long black whiskers, who was waving his arms and delivering an excited but succinct harangue. Key and Rose, having wedged themselves into the approximate parquet, scrutinized him with acute suspicion, as his words penetrated their common consciousness.

"—What have you got outta the war?" he was crying fiercely. "Look arounja, look arounja! Are you rich? Have you got a lot of money offered you?—no; you're lucky if you're alive and got both your legs; you're lucky if you came back an' find your wife ain't gone off with some other fella that had the money to buy himself out of the war! That's when you're lucky! Who got anything out of it except J. P. Morgan an' John D. Rockerfeller?"

At this point the little Jew's oration was interrupted by the hostile impact of a fist upon the point of his bearded chin and he toppled backward to a sprawl on the pavement.

"God damn Bolsheviki!" cried the big soldier-blacksmith who had delivered the blow. There was a rumble of approval, the crowd closed in nearer.

The Jew staggered to his feet, and immediately went down again before a half-dozen reaching-in fists. This time he stayed down, breathing heavily, blood oozing from his lip where it was cut within and without.

There was a riot of voices, and in a minute Rose and Key found themselves flowing with the jumbled crowd down Sixth Avenue under the leadership of a thin civilian in a slouch hat and the brawny soldier who had summarily ended the oration. The crowd had marvellously swollen to formidable proportions and a stream of more non-committal citizens followed it along the sidewalks lending their moral support by intermittent huzzas.

"Where we goin'?" yelled Key to the man nearest him.

His neighbor pointed up to the leader in the slouch hat.

"That guy knows where there's a lot of 'em! We're goin' to show 'em!"

"We're goin' to show 'em!" whispered Key delightedly to Rose, who repeated the phrase rapturously to a man on the other side.

Down Sixth Avenue swept the procession, joined here and there by soldiers and marines, and now and then by civilians, who came up with the inevitable cry that they were just out of the army themselves, as if presenting it as a card of admission to a newly formed Sporting and Amusement Club.

Then the procession swerved down a cross street and headed for Fifth Avenue and the word filtered here and there that they were bound for a Red meeting at Tolliver Hall.

"Where is it?"

The question went up the line and a moment later the answer floated back. Tolliver Hall was down on Tenth Street. There was a bunch of other sojers who was goin' to break it up and was down there now!

But Tenth Street had a faraway sound and at the word a general groan went up and a score of the procession dropped out. Among these were Rose and Key, who slowed down to a saunter and let the more enthusiastic sweep on by.

"I'd rather get some liquor," said Key as they halted and made their way to the sidewalk amid cries of "Shell hole!" and "Quitters!"

"Does your brother work around here?" asked Rose, assuming the air of one passing from the superficial to the eternal.

"He oughta," replied Key. "I ain't seen him for a coupla years. I been out to Pennsylvania since. Maybe he don't work at night anyhow. It's right along here. He can get us some o'right if he ain't gone."

They found the place after a few minutes' patrol of the street—a shoddy tablecloth restaurant between Fifth Avenue and Broadway. Here Key went inside to inquire for his brother George, while Rose waited on the sidewalk.

"He ain't here no more," said Key emerging. "He's a waiter up to Delmonico's."

Rose nodded wisely, as if he'd expected as much. One should not be surprised at a capable man changing jobs occasionally. He knew a waiter once— there ensued a long conversation as they walked as to whether waiters made more in actual wages than in tips—it was decided that it depended on the social tone of the joint wherein the waiter labored. After having given each other vivid pictures of millionaires dining at Delmonico's and throwing away fifty-dollar bills after their first quart of champagne, both men thought privately of becoming waiters. In fact, Key's narrow brow was secreting a resolution to ask his brother to get him a job.

"A waiter can drink up all the champagne those fellas leave in bottles," suggested Rose with some relish, and then added as an afterthought, "Oh, boy!"

By the time they reached Delmonico's it was half past ten, and they were surprised to see a stream of taxis driving up to the door one after the other and emitting marvelous, hatless young ladies, each one attended by a stiff young gentleman in evening clothes.

"It's a party," said Rose with some awe. "Maybe we better not go in. He'll be busy."

"No, he won't. He'll be o'right."

After some hesitation they entered what appeared

to them to be the least elaborate door and, indecision falling upon them immediately, stationed themselves nervously in an inconspicuous corner of the small dining room in which they found themselves. They took off their caps and held them in their hands. A cloud of gloom fell upon them and both started when a door at one end of the room crashed open, emitting a comet-like waiter who streaked across the floor and vanished through another door on the other side.

There had been three of these lightning passages before the seekers mustered the acumen to hail a waiter. He turned, looked at them suspiciously, and then approached with soft, catlike steps, as if prepared at any moment to turn and flee.

"Say," began Key, "say, do you know my brother? He's a waiter here."

"His name is Key," annotated Rose.

Yes, the waiter knew Key. He was upstairs, he thought. There was a big dance going on in the main ballroom. He'd tell him.

Ten minutes later George Key appeared and greeted his brother with the utmost suspicion; his first and most natural thought being that he was going to be asked for money.

George was tall and weak chinned, but there his resemblance to his brother ceased. The waiter's eyes were not dull, they were alert and twinkling, and his manner was suave, indoor, and faintly superior. They exchanged formalities. George was married and had three children. He seemed fairly interested, but not impressed by the news that Carrol had been abroad in the army. This disappointed Carrol.

"George," said the younger brother, these amenities having been disposed of, "we want to get some booze, and they won't sell us none. Can you get us some?"

George considered.

"Sure. Maybe I can. It may be half an hour, though."

"All right," agreed Carrol, "we'll wait."

At this Rose started to sit down in a convenient chair, but was hailed to his feet by the indignant George.

"Hey! Watch out, you! Can't sit down here! This room's all set for a twelve o'clock banquet."

"I ain't goin' to hurt it," said Rose resentfully. "I been through the delouser."

"Never mind," said George sternly, "if the head waiter seen me here talkin' he'd romp all over me."

"Oh."

The mention of the head waiter was full explanation to the other two; they fingered their overseas caps nervously and waited for a suggestion.

"I tell you," said George, after a pause, "I got a place you can wait; you just come here with me."

They followed him out the far door, through a deserted pantry and up a pair of dark winding stairs, emerging finally into a small room chiefly furnished by piles of pails and stacks of scrubbing brushes, and illuminated by a single dim electric light. There he left them, after soliciting two dollars and agreeing to return in half an hour with a quart of whiskey.

"George is makin' money, I bet," said Key gloomily as he seated himself on an inverted pail. "I bet he's making fifty dollars a week."

Rose nodded his head and spat.

"I bet he is, too."

"What'd he say the dance was of?"

"A lot of college fellas. Yale College."

They both nodded solemnly at each other.

"Wonder where that crowd a sojers is now?"

"I don't know. I know that's too damn long to walk for me."

"Me too. You don't catch me walkin' that far."

Ten minutes later restlessness seized them.

"I'm goin' to see what's out here," said Rose, stepping cautiously toward the other door.

It was a swinging door of green baize and he pushed it open a cautious inch.

"See anything?"

For answer Rose drew in his breath sharply.

"Doggone! Here's some liquor I'll say!"

"Liquor?"

Key joined Rose at the door, and looked eagerly.

"I'll tell the world that's liquor," he said, after a moment of concentrated gazing.

It was a room about twice as large as the one they were in—and in it was prepared a radiant feast of spirits. There were long walls of alternating bottles set along two white covered tables; whiskey, gin, brandy, French and Italian vermouths, and orange juice, not to mention an array of syphons and two great empty punch bowls. The room was as yet uninhabited.

"It's for this dance they're just starting," whispered Key; "hear the violins playin'? Say, boy, I wouldn't mind havin' a dance."

They closed the door softly and exchanged a glance of mutual comprehension. There was no need of feeling each other out.

"I'd like to get my hands on a coupla those bottles," said Rose emphatically.

"Me too."

"Do you suppose we'd get seen?"

Key considered.

"Maybe we better wait till they start drinkin' 'em. They got 'em all laid out now, and they know how many of them there are."

They debated this point for several minutes. Rose was all for getting his hands on a bottle now and tucking it under his coat before any one came into the room. Key, however, advocated caution. He was afraid he might get his brother in trouble. If they waited till some of the bottles were opened it'd be all right to take one, and everybody'd think it was one of the college fellas.

While they were still engaged in argument George Key hurried through the room and, barely grunting at them, disappeared by way of the green baize door. A minute later they heard several corks pop, and then the sound of cracking ice and splashing liquid. George was mixing the punch.

The soldiers exchanged delighted grins.

"Oh, boy!" whispered Rose.

George reappeared.

"Just keep low, boys," he said quickly. "I'll have your stuff for you in five minutes."

He disappeared through the door by which he had come.

As soon as his footsteps receded down the stairs, Rose, after a cautious look, darted into the room of delights and reappeared with a bottle in his hand.

"Here's what I say," he said, as they sat radiantly digesting their first drink. "We'll wait till he comes up, and we'll ask him if we can't just stay here and drink what he brings us—see. We'll tell him we haven't got any place to drink it—see. Then we can sneak in there whenever there ain't nobody in that there room and tuck a bottle under our coats. We'll have enough to last us a coupla days—see?"

"Sure," agreed Rose enthusiastically. "Oh, boy! And if we want to we can sell it to sojers any time we want to."

They were silent for a moment thinking rosily of this idea. Then Key reached up and unhooked the collar of his O. D. coat.

"It's hot in here, ain't it?"

Rose agreed earnestly.

"Hot as hell."

IV She was still quite angry when she came out of the
dressing room and crossed the intervening parlor of
politeness that opened onto the hall—angry not so
much at the actual happening which was, after all,
the merest commonplace of her social existence, but
because it had occurred on this particular night. She
had no quarrel with herself. She had acted with that
correct mixture of dignity and reticent pity which
she always employed. She had succinctly and deftly
snubbed him.

It had happened when their taxi was leaving the
Biltmore—hadn't gone half a block. He had lifted his
right arm awkwardly—she was on his right side—and
attempted to settle it snugly around the crimson fur-
trimmed opera cloak she wore. This in itself had been

a mistake. It was inevitably more graceful for a young man attempting to embrace a young lady of whose acquiescence he was not certain, to first put his far arm around her. It avoided that awkward movement of raising the near arm.

His second *faux pas* was unconscious. She had spent the afternoon at the hairdresser's; the idea of any calamity overtaking her hair was extremely repugnant—yet as Peter made his unfortunate attempt the point of his elbow had just faintly brushed it. That was his second *faux pas*. Two were quite enough.

He had begun to murmur. At the first murmur she had decided that he was nothing but a college boy— Edith was twenty-two, and anyhow, this dance, first of its kind since the war, was reminding her, with the accelerating rhythm of its associations, of something else—of another dance and another man, a man for whom her feelings had been little more than a sad-eyed, adolescent mooniness. Edith Bradin was falling in love with her recollection of Gordon Sterrett.

So she came out of the dressing room at Delmonico's and stood for a second in the doorway looking over the shoulders of a black dress in front of her at the groups of Yale men who flitted like dignified black moths around the head of the stairs. From the room she had left drifted out the heavy fragrance left by the passage to and fro of many scented young beauties—rich perfumes and the fragile memory-laden dust of fragrant powders. This odor drifting out acquired the tang of cigarette smoke in the hall, and then settled sensuously down the stairs and permeated the ballroom where the Gamma Psi dance was to be held. It was an odor she knew well, exciting, stimulating, restlessly sweet—the odor of a fashionable dance.

She thought of her own appearance. Her bare arms and shoulders were powdered to a creamy white. She knew they looked very soft and would gleam like milk against the black backs that were to silhouette them tonight. The hairdressing had been a success; her reddish mass of hair was piled and crushed and creased to an arrogant marvel of mobile curves. Her lips were finely made of deep carmine; the irises of her eyes were delicate, breakable blue, like china eyes. She was a complete, infinitely delicate, quite perfect thing of beauty, flowing in an even line from a complex coiffure to two small slim feet.

She thought of what she would say tonight at this revel, faintly prestiged already by the sounds of high and low laughter and slippered footsteps, and movements of couples up and down the stairs. She would talk the language she had talked for many years—her line—made up of the current expressions, bits of journalese and college slang strung together into an intrinsic whole, careless, faintly provocative, delicately sentimental. She smiled faintly as she heard a girl sitting on the stairs near her say: "You don't know the half of it, dearie!"

And as she smiled her anger melted for a moment,

and closing her eyes she drew in a deep breath of pleasure. She dropped her arms to her side until they were faintly touching the sleek sheath that covered and suggested her figure. She had never felt her own softness so much nor so enjoyed the whiteness of her own arms.

"I smell sweet," she said to herself simply, and then came another thought—"I'm made for love."

She liked the sound of this and thought it again; then in inevitable succession came her newborn riot of dreams about Gordon. The twist of her imagination which, two months before, had disclosed to her her unguessed desire to see him again, seemed now to have been leading up to this dance, this hour.

For all her sleek beauty, Edith was a grave, slow-thinking girl. There was a streak in her of that same desire to ponder, of that adolescent idealism that had turned her brother socialist and pacifist. Henry Bradin had left Cornell, where he had been an instructor in economics, and had come to New York to pour the latest cures for incurable evils into the columns of a radical weekly newspaper.

Edith, less fatuously, would have been content to cure Gordon Sterrett. There was a quality of weakness in Gordon that she wanted to take care of; there was a helplessness in him that she wanted to protect. And she wanted someone she had known a long while, someone who had loved her a long while. She was a little tired; she wanted to get married. Out of a pile of letters, half a dozen pictures and as many memories, and this weariness, she had decided that next time she saw Gordon their relations were going to be changed. She would say something that would change them. There was this evening. This was her evening. All evenings were her evenings.

Then her thoughts were interrupted by a solemn undergraduate with a hurt look and an air of strained formality who presented himself before her and bowed unusually low. It was the man she had come with, Peter Himmel. He was tall and humorous, with horned-rimmed glasses and an air of attractive whimsicality. She suddenly rather disliked him— probably because he had not succeeded in kissing her.

"Well," she began, "are you still furious at me?"

"Not at all."

She stepped forward and took his arm.

"I'm sorry," she said softly. "I don't know why I snapped out that way. I'm in a bum humor tonight for some strange reason. I'm sorry."

"S'all right," he mumbled, "don't mention it."

He felt disagreeably embarrassed. Was she rubbing in the fact of his late failure?

"It was a mistake," she continued, on the same consciously gentle key. "We'll both forget it." For this he hated her.

A few minutes later they drifted out on the floor while the dozen swaying, sighing members of the specially hired jazz orchestra informed the crowded ballroom that "if a saxophone and me are left alone why then two is com-pan-ee!"

A man with a mustache cut in. "Hello," he began reprovingly. "You don't remember me."

"I can't just think of your name," she said lightly—"and I know you so well."

"I met you up at—" His voice trailed disconsolately off as a man with very fair hair cut in. Edith murmured a conventional "Thanks, loads—cut in later," to the *inconnu*.

The very fair man insisted on shaking hands enthusiastically. She placed him as one of the numerous Jims of her acquaintance—last name a mystery. She remembered even that he had a peculiar rhythm in dancing and found as they started that she was right.

"Going to be here long?" he breathed confidentially.

She leaned back and looked up at him.

"Couple of weeks."

"Where are you?"

"Biltmore. Call me up some day."

"I mean it," he assured her. "I will. We'll go to tea."

"So do I—Do."

A dark man cut in with intense formality.

"You don't remember me, do you?" he said gravely.

"I should say I do. Your name's Harlan."

"No-ope. Barlow."

"Well, I knew there were two syllables anyway. You're the boy that played the ukulele so well up at Howard Marshall's house party."

"I played—but not—"

A man with prominent teeth cut in. Edith inhaled a slight cloud of whiskey. She liked men to have had something to drink; they were so much more cheerful, and appreciative and complimentary—much easier to talk to.

"My name's Dean, Philip Dean," he said cheerfully. "You don't remember me, I know, but you used to come up to New Haven with a fellow I roomed with senior year, Gordon Sterrett."

Edith looked up quickly.

"Yes, I went up with him twice—to the Pump and Slipper and the Junior prom."

"You've seen him, of course," said Dean carelessly. "He's here tonight. I saw him just a minute ago."

Edith started. Yet she had felt quite sure he would be here.

"Why, no, I haven't—"

A fat man with red hair cut in.

"Hello, Edith," he began.

"Why—hello there—"

She slipped, stumbled lightly.

"I'm sorry, dear," she murmured mechanically.

She had seen Gordon—Gordon very white and listless, leaning against the side of a doorway, smoking and looking into the ballroom. Edith could see that his face was thin and wan—that the hand he raised to his lips with a cigarette was trembling. They were dancing quite close to him now.

"—They invite so darn many extra fellas that you—" the short man was saying.

"Hello, Gordon," called Edith over her partner's shoulder. Her heart was pounding wildly.

His large dark eyes were fixed on her. He took a step in her direction. Her partner turned her away—she heard his voice bleating—

"—but half the stags get lit and leave before long, so—"

Then a low tone at her side.

"May I, please?"

She was dancing suddenly with Gordon; one of his arms was around her; she felt it tighten spasmodically; felt his hand on her back with the fingers spread. Her hand holding the little lace handkerchief was crushed in his.

"Why Gordon," she began breathlessly.

"Hello, Edith."

She slipped again—was tossed forward by her recovery until her face touched the black cloth of his dinner coat. She loved him—she knew she loved him—then for a minute there was silence while a strange feeling of uneasiness crept over her. Something was wrong.

Of a sudden her heart wrenched, and turned over as she realized what it was. He was pitiful and wretched, a little drunk, and miserably tired.

"Oh—" she cried involuntarily.

His eyes looked down at her. She saw suddenly that they were blood-streaked and rolling uncontrollably.

"Gordon," she murmured, "we'll sit down; I want to sit down."

They were nearly in mid-floor, but she had seen two men start toward her from opposite sides of the room, so she halted, seized Gordon's limp hand and led him bumping through the crowd, her mouth tight shut, her face a little pale under her rouge, her eyes trembling with tears.

She found a place high up on the soft-carpeted stairs, and he sat down heavily beside her.

"Well," he began, staring at her unsteadily, "I certainly am glad to see you, Edith."

She looked at him without answering. The effect of this on her was immeasurable. For years she had seen men in various stages of intoxication, from uncles all the way down to chauffeurs, and her feelings had varied from amusement to disgust, but here for the first time she was seized with a new feeling—an unutterable horror.

"Gordon," she said accusingly and almost crying, "you look like the devil."

He nodded. "I've had trouble, Edith."

"Trouble?"

"All sorts of trouble. Don't you say anything to the family, but I'm all gone to pieces. I'm a mess, Edith."

His lower lip was sagging. He seemed scarcely to see her.

"Can't you—can't you," she hesitated, "can't you tell me about it, Gordon? You know I'm always interested in you."

She bit her lip—she had intended to say something stronger, but found at the end that she couldn't bring it out.

Gordon shook his head dully. "I can't tell you. You're a good woman. I can't tell a good woman the story."

"Rot," she said, defiantly. "I think it's a perfect insult to call any one a good woman in that way. It's a slam. You've been drinking, Gordon."

"Thanks." He inclined his head gravely. "Thanks for the information."

"Why do you drink?"

"Because I'm so damn miserable."

"Do you think drinking's going to make it any better?"

"What you doing—trying to reform me?"

"No; I'm trying to help you, Gordon. Can't you tell me about it?"

"I'm in an awful mess. Best thing you can do is to pretend not to know me."

"Why, Gordon?"

"I'm sorry I cut in on you—it's unfair to you. You're pure woman—and all that sort of thing. Here, I'll get someone else to dance with you."

He rose clumsily to his feet, but she reached up and pulled him down beside her on the stairs.

"Here, Gordon. You're ridiculous. You're hurting me. You're acting like a—like a crazy man—"

"I admit it. I'm a little crazy. Something's wrong with me, Edith. There's something left me. It doesn't matter."

"It does, tell me."

"Just that. I was always queer—little bit different from other boys. All right in college, but now it's all wrong. Things have been snapping inside me for four months like little hooks on a dress, and it's about to come off when a few more hooks go. I'm very gradually going loony."

He turned his eyes full on her and began to laugh, and she shrank away from him.

"What *is* the matter?"

"Just me," he repeated. "I'm going loony. This whole place is like a dream to me—this Delmonico's—"

As he talked she saw he had changed utterly. He wasn't at all light and gay and careless—a great lethargy and discouragement had come over him. Revulsion seized her, followed by a faint, surprising boredom. His voice seemed to come out of a great void.

"Edith," he said, "I used to think I was clever, talented, an artist. Now I know I'm nothing. Can't draw, Edith. Don't know why I'm telling you this."

She nodded absently.

"I can't draw, I can't do anything. I'm poor as a church mouse." He laughed, bitterly and rather too loud. "I've become a damn beggar, a leech on my friends. I'm a failure. I'm poor as hell."

Her distaste was growing. She barely nodded this time, waiting for her first possible cue to rise.

Suddenly Gordon's eyes filled with tears.

"Edith," he said, turning to her with what was evidently a strong effort at self-control, "I can't tell you what it means to me to know there's one person left who's interested in me."

He reached out and patted her hand, and involuntarily she drew it away.

"It's mighty fine of you," he repeated.

"Well," she said slowly, looking him in the eye, "anyone's always glad to see an old friend—but I'm sorry to see you like this, Gordon."

There was a pause while they looked at each other, and the momentary eagerness in his eyes wavered. She rose and stood looking at him, her face quite expressionless.

"Shall we dance?" she suggested, coolly.

—Love is fragile—she was thinking—but perhaps the pieces are saved, the things that hovered on lips, that might have been said. The new love words, the tendernesses learned, are treasured up for the next lover.

V Peter Himmel, escort to the lovely Edith, was unaccustomed to being snubbed; having been snubbed, he was hurt and embarrassed, and ashamed of himself. For a matter of two months he had been on special delivery terms with Edith Bradin, and knowing that the one excuse and explanation of the special delivery letter is its value in sentimental correspondence, he had believed himself quite sure of his ground. He searched in vain for any reason why she should have taken this attitude in the matter of a simple kiss.

Therefore when he was cut in on by the man with the mustache he went out into the hall and, making up a sentence, said it over to himself several times. Considerably deleted, this was it:

"Well, if any girl ever led a man on and then jolted him, she did—and she has no kick coming if I go out and get beautifully boiled."

So he walked through the supper room into a small room adjoining it, which he had located earlier in the evening. It was a room in which there were several large bowls of punch flanked by many bottles. He took a seat beside the table which held the bottles.

At the second highball, boredom, disgust, the monotony of time, the turbidity of events, sank into a vague background before which glittering cobwebs formed. Things became reconciled to themselves, things lay quietly on their shelves; the troubles of the day arranged themselves in trim formation and at his curt wish of dismissal, marched off and disappeared. And with the departure of worry came brilliant, permeating symbolism. Edith became a flighty, negligible girl, not to be worried over; rather to be laughed at. She fitted like a figure of his own dream into the surface world forming about him. He himself became in a measure symbolic, a type of the continent bacchanal, the brilliant dreamer at play.

Then the symbolic mood faded and as he sipped his third highball his imagination yielded to the warm glow and he lapsed into a state similar to floating on his back in pleasant water. It was at this point that he noticed that a green baize door near him was open about two inches, and that through the aperture a pair of eyes were watching him intently.

"Hm," murmured Peter calmly.

The green door closed—and then opened again—a bare half inch this time.

"Peek-a-boo," murmured Peter.

The door remained stationary and then he became aware of a series of tense intermittent whispers.

"One guy."

"What's he doin'?"

"He's sittin' lookin'."

"He better beat it off. We gotta get another li'l' bottle."

Peter listened while the words filtered into his consciousness.

"Now this," he thought, "is most remarkable."

He was excited. He was jubilant. He felt that he had stumbled upon a mystery. Affecting an elaborate carelessness he arose and walked around the table—then, turning quickly, pulled open the green door, precipitating Private Rose into the room.

Peter bowed.

"How do you do?" he said.

Private Rose set one foot slightly in front of the other, poised for fight, flight, or compromise

"How do you do?" repeated Peter politely.

"I'm o'right."

"Can I offer you a drink?"

Private Rose looked at him searchingly, suspecting possible sarcasm.

"O'right," he said finally.

Peter indicated a chair.

"Sit down."

"I got a friend," said Rose, "I got a friend in there." He pointed to the green door.

"By all means let's have him in."

Peter crossed over, opened the door and welcomed in Private Key, very suspicious and uncertain and guilty. Chairs were found and the three took their seats around the punch bowl. Peter gave them each a highball and offered them a cigarette from his case. They accepted both with some diffidence.

"Now," continued Peter easily, "may I ask why you gentlemen prefer to lounge away your leisure hours in a room which is chiefly furnished, as far as I can see, with scrubbing brushes. And when the human race has progressed to the stage where seventeen thousand chairs are manufactured on every day except Sunday—" he paused. Rose and Key regarded him vacantly. "Will you tell me," went on Peter, "why you choose to rest yourselves on articles intended for the transportation of water from one place to another?"

At this point Rose contributed a grunt to the conversation.

"And lastly," finished Peter, "will you tell me why, when you are in a building beautifully hung with enormous candelabra, you prefer to spend these evening hours under one anemic electric light?"

Rose looked at Key; Key looked at Rose. They laughed; they laughed uproariously; they found it was impossible to look at each other without laughing.

But they were not laughing with this man—they were laughing at him. To them a man who talked after this fashion was either raving drunk or raving crazy.

"You are Yale men, I presume," said Peter, finishing his highball and preparing another.

They laughed again.

"Na-ah."

"So? I thought perhaps you might be members of that lowly section of the university known as the Sheffield Scientific School."

"Na-ah."

"Hm. Well, that's too bad. No doubt you are Harvard men, anxious to preserve your incognito in this—this paradise of violet blue, as the newspapers say."

"Na-ah," said Key scornfully, "we was just waitin' for somebody."

"Ah," exclaimed Peter, rising and filling their glasses, "very interestin'. Had a date with a scrublady, eh?"

They both denied this indignantly.

"It's all right," Peter reassured them, "don't apologize. A scrublady's as good as any lady in the world. Kipling says 'Any lady and Judy O'Grady under the skin.'"

"Sure," said Key, winking broadly at Rose.

"My case, for instance," continued Peter, finishing his glass. "I got a girl up here that's spoiled. Spoildest darn girl I ever saw. Refused to kiss me; no reason whatsoever. Led me on deliberately to think sure I want to kiss you and then plunk! Threw me over! What's the younger generation comin' to?"

"Say tha's hard luck," said Key—"that's awful hard luck."

"Oh, boy!" said Rose.

"Have another?" said Peter.

"We got in a sort of fight for a while," said Key after a pause, "but it was too far away."

"A fight?—tha's stuff!" said Peter, seating himself unsteadily. "Fight 'em all! I was in the army."

"This was with a Bolshevik fella."

"Tha's stuff!" exclaimed Peter, enthusiastic. "That's what I say! Kill the Bolshevik! Exterminate 'em!"

"We're Americuns," said Rose, implying a sturdy, defiant patriotism.

"Sure," said Peter. "Greatest race in the world! We're all Americuns! Have another."

They had another.

VI At one o'clock a special orchestra, special even in a day of special orchestras, arrived at Delmonico's, and its members, seating themselves arrogantly around the piano, took up the burden of providing music for the Gamma Psi Fraternity. They were headed by a famous flute-player, distinguished throughout New York for his feat of standing on his head and shimmying with his shoulders while he played the latest jazz on his flute. During his performance the lights were extinguished except for the spotlight on the flute-player and another roving beam that threw flickering shadows and changing kaleidoscopic colors over the massed dancers.

Edith had danced herself into that tired, dreamy state habitual only with debutantes, a state equivalent to the glow of a noble soul after several long highballs. Her mind floated vaguely on the bosom of her music; her partners changed with the unreality of phantoms under the colorful shifting dusk, and to her present coma it seemed as if days had passed since the dance began. She had talked on many fragmentary subjects with many men. She had been kissed once and made love to six times. Earlier in the evening different undergraduates had danced with her, but now, like all the more popular girls there, she had her own entourage—that is, half a dozen gallants had singled her out or were alternating her charms with those of some other chosen beauty; they cut in on her in regular, inevitable succession.

Several times she had seen Gordon—he had been sitting a long time on the stairway with his palm to his head, his dull eyes fixed at an infinite speck on the floor before him, very depressed, he looked, and quite drunk—but Edith each time had averted her glance hurriedly. All that seemed long ago; her mind was passive now, her senses were lulled to trancelike sleep; only her feet danced and her voice talked on in hazy sentimental banter.

But Edith was not nearly so tired as to be incapable of moral indignation when Peter Himmel cut in on her, sublimely and happily drunk. She gasped and looked up at him.

"Why, *Peter*!"

"I'm a li'l' stewed, Edith."

"Why, Peter, you're a *peach*, you are! Don't you

think it's a bum way of doing—when you're with me?"

Then she smiled unwillingly, for he was looking at her with owlish sentimentality varied with a silly spasmodic smile.

"Darlin' Edith," he began earnestly, "you know I love you, don't you?"

"You tell it well."

"I love you—and I merely wanted you to kiss me," he added sadly.

His embarrassment, his shame, were both gone. She was a mos' beautiful girl in whole worl'. Mos' beautiful eyes, like stars above. He wanted to 'pologize—firs', for presuming try to kiss her; second, for drinking—but he'd been so discouraged 'cause he had thought she was mad at him—

The red-fat man cut in, and looking up at Edith smiled radiantly.

"Did you bring anyone?" she asked.

No. The red-fat man was a stag.

"Well, would you mind—would it be an awful bother for you to—to take me home tonight?" (this extreme diffidence was a charming affectation on Edith's part—she knew that the red-fat man would immediately dissolve into a paroxysm of delight).

"Bother? Why, good Lord, I'd be darn glad to! You know I'd be darn glad to."

"Thanks *loads*! You're awfully sweet."

She glanced at her wristwatch. It was half past one. And, as she said "half past one" to herself, it floated vaguely into her mind that her brother had told her at luncheon that he worked in the office of his newspaper until after one-thirty every evening.

Edith turned suddenly to her current partner.

"What street is Delmonico's on, anyway?"

"Street? Oh, why Fifth Avenue, of course."

"I mean, what cross street?"

"Why—let's see—it's on Forty-fourth Street."

This verified what she had thought. Henry's office must be across the street and just around the corner, and it occurred to her immediately that she might slip over for a moment and surprise him, float in on him, a shimmering marvel in her new crimson opera cloak and "cheer him up." It was exactly the sort of thing Edith revelled in doing—an unconventional, jaunty thing. The idea reached out and gripped at her imagination—after an instant's hesitation she had decided.

"My hair is just about to tumble entirely down," she said pleasantly to her partner; "would you mind if I go and fix it?"

"Not at all."

"You're a peach."

A few minutes later, wrapped in her crimson opera cloak, she flitted down a side-stairs, her cheeks glowing with excitement at her little adventure. She ran by a couple who stood at the door—a weak-chinned waiter and an over-rouged young lady, in hot dispute—and opening the outer door stepped into the warm May night.

VII

The over-rouged young lady followed her with a brief, bitter glance—then turned again to the weak-chinned waiter and took up her argument.

"You better go up and tell him I'm here," she said defiantly, "or I'll go up myself."

"No, you don't!" said George sternly.

The girl smiled sardonically.

"Oh, I don't, don't I? Well, let me tell you I know more college fellas and more of 'em know me, and are glad to take me out on a party, than you ever saw in your whole life."

"Maybe so—"

"Maybe so," she interrupted. "Oh, it's all right for any of 'em like that one that just ran out—God knows where *she* went—it's all right for them that are asked here to come or go as they like—but when I want to see a friend they have some cheap, ham-slinging, bring-me-a-doughnut waiter to stand here and keep me out."

"See here," said the elder Key indignantly, "I can't lose my job. Maybe this fella you're talkin' about doesn't want to see you."

"Oh, he wants to see me all right."

"Anyways, how could I find him in all that crowd?"

"Oh, he'll be there," she asserted confidently. "You just ask anybody for Gordon Sterrett and they'll point him out to you. They all know each other, those fellas."

She produced a mesh bag, and taking out a dollar bill handed it to George.

"Here," she said, "here's a bribe. You find him and give him my message. You tell him if he isn't here in five minutes I'm coming up."

George shook his head pessimistically, considered the question for a moment, wavered violently, and then withdrew.

In less than the allotted time Gordon came downstairs. He was drunker than he had been earlier in the evening and in a different way. The liquor seemed to have hardened on him like a crust. He was heavy and lurching—almost incoherent when he talked.

"'Lo, Jewel," he said thickly. "Came right away. Jewel, I couldn't get that money. Tried my best."

"Money nothing!" she snapped. "You haven't been near me for ten days. What's the matter?"

He shook his head slowly.

"Been very low, Jewel. Been sick."

"Why didn't you tell me if you were sick. I don't care about the money that bad. I didn't start bothering you about it at all until you began neglecting me."

Again he shook his head.

"Haven't been neglecting you. Not at all."

"Haven't! You haven't been near me for three weeks, unless you been so drunk you didn't know what you were doing."

"Been sick, Jewel," he repeated, turning his eyes upon her wearily.

"You're well enough to come and play with your society friends here all right. You told me you'd meet me for dinner, and you said you'd have some money for me. You didn't even bother to ring me up."

"I couldn't get any money."

"Haven't I just been saying that doesn't matter? I wanted to see you, Gordon, but you seem to prefer your somebody else."

He denied this bitterly.

"Then get your hat and come along," she suggested.

Gordon hesitated—and she came suddenly close to him and slipped her arms around his neck.

"Come on with me, Gordon," she said in a half whisper. "We'll go over to Devineries' and have a drink, and then we can go up to my apartment."

"I can't, Jewel,—"

"You can," she said intensely.

"I'm sick as a dog!"

"Well, then, you oughtn't to stay here and dance."

With a glance around him in which relief and despair were mingled, Gordon hesitated; then she suddenly pulled him to her and kissed him with soft, pulpy lips.

"All right," he said heavily. "I'll get my hat."

VIII

When Edith came out into the clear blue of the May night she found the Avenue deserted. The windows of the big shops were dark; over their doors were drawn great iron masks until they were only shadowy tombs of the late day's splendor. Glancing down toward Forty-second Street she saw a commingled blur of lights from the all-night restaurants. Over on Sixth Avenue the elevated, a flare of fire, roared across the street between the glimmering parallels of light at the station and streaked along into the crisp dark. But at Forty-fourth Street it was very quiet.

Pulling her cloak close about her Edith darted across the Avenue. She started nervously as a solitary man passed her and said in a hoarse whisper—"Where bound, kiddo?" She was reminded of a night in her childhood when she had walked around the block in her pajamas and a dog had howled at her from a mystery-big backyard.

In a minute she had reached her destination, a two-story, comparatively old building on Forty-fourth, in the upper window of which she thankfully detected a wisp of light. It was bright enough outside for her to make out the sign beside the window—the *New York Trumpet*. She stepped inside a dark hall and after a second saw the stairs in the corner.

Then she was in a long, low room furnished with many desks and hung on all sides with file copies of newspapers. There were only two occupants. They were sitting at different ends of the room, each wearing a green eye-shade and writing by a solitary desk light.

For a moment she stood uncertainly in the doorway, and then both men turned around simultaneously and she recognized her brother.

"Why, Edith!" He rose quickly and approached her in surprise, removing his eye-shade. He was tall, lean, and dark, with black, piercing eyes under very thick glasses. They were far-away eyes that seemed always fixed just over the head of the person to whom he was talking.

He put his hands on her arms and kissed her cheek.

"What is it?" he repeated in some alarm.

"I was at a dance across at Delmonico's, Henry," she said excitedly, "and I couldn't resist tearing over to see you."

"I'm glad you did." His alertness gave way

quickly to a habitual vagueness. "You oughtn't to be out alone at night though, ought you?"

The man at the other end of the room had been looking at them curiously, but at Henry's beckoning gesture he approached. He was loosely fat with little twinkling eyes, and, having removed his collar and tie, he gave the impression of a Middle-Western farmer on a Sunday afternoon.

"This is my sister," said Henry. "She dropped in to see me."

"How do you do?" said the fat man, smiling. "My name's Bartholomew, Miss Bradin. I know your brother has forgotten it long ago."

Edith laughed politely.

"Well," he continued, "not exactly gorgeous quarters we have here, are they?"

Edith looked around the room.

"They seem very nice," she replied. "Where do you keep the bombs?"

"The bombs?" repeated Bartholomew, laughing. "That's pretty good—the bombs. Did you hear her, Henry? She wants to know where we keep the bombs. Say, that's pretty good."

Edith swung herself onto a vacant desk and sat dangling her feet over the edge. Her brother took a seat beside her.

"Well," he asked, absent-mindedly, "how do you like New York this trip?"

"Not bad. I'll be over at the Biltmore with the Hoyts until Sunday. Can't you come to luncheon tomorrow?"

He thought a moment.

"I'm especially busy," he objected, "and I hate women in groups."

"All right," she agreed, unruffled. "Let's you and me have luncheon together."

"Very well."

"I'll call for you at twelve."

Bartholomew was obviously anxious to return to his desk, but apparently considered that it would be rude to leave without some parting pleasantry.

"Well"—he began awkwardly.

They both turned to him.

"Well, we—we had an exciting time earlier in the evening."

The two men exchanged glances.

"You should have come earlier," continued Bartholomew, somewhat encouraged. "We had a regular vaudeville."

"Did you really?"

"A serenade," said Henry. "A lot of soldiers gathered down there in the street and began to yell at the sign."

"Why?" she demanded.

"Just a crowd," said Henry, abstractedly. "All crowds have to howl. They didn't have anybody with much initiative in the lead, or they'd probably have forced their way in here and smashed things up."

"Yes," said Bartholomew, turning again to Edith, "you should have been here."

He seemed to consider this a sufficient cue for withdrawal, for he turned abruptly and went back to his desk.

"Are the soldiers all set against the Socialists?" demanded Edith of her brother. "I mean do they attack you violently and all that?"

Henry replaced his eye-shade and yawned.

"The human race has come a long way," he said casually, "but most of us are throwbacks; the soldiers don't know what they want, or what they hate, or what they like. They're used to acting in large bodies, and they seem to have to make demonstrations. So it happens to be against us. There've been riots all over the city tonight. It's May Day, you see."

"Was the disturbance here pretty serious?"

"Not a bit," he said scornfully. "About twenty-five of them stopped in the street about nine o'clock, and began to bellow at the moon."

"Oh"—She changed the subject. "You're glad to see me, Henry?"

"Why, sure."

"You don't seem to be."

"I am."

"I suppose you think I'm a—a waster. Sort of the World's Worst Butterfly."

Henry laughed.

"Not at all. Have a good time while you're young. Why? Do I seem like the priggish and earnest youth?"

"No—" She paused, "—but somehow I began thinking how absolutely different the party I'm on is from—from all your purposes. It seems sort of—of incongruous, doesn't it?—me being at a party like that, and you over here working for a thing that'll make that sort of party impossible ever any more, if your ideas work."

"I don't think of it that way. You're young, and you're acting just as you were brought up to act. Go ahead—have a good time?"

Her feet, which had been idly swinging, stopped and her voice dropped a note.

"I wish you'd—you'd come back to Harrisburg and have a good time. Do you feel sure that you're on the right track—"

"You're wearing beautiful stockings," he interrupted. "What on earth are they?"

"They're embroidered," she replied, glancing down. "Aren't they cunning?" She raised her skirts and uncovered slim, silk-sheathed calves. "Or do you disapprove of silk stockings?"

He seemed slightly exasperated, bent his dark eyes on her piercingly.

"Are you trying to make me out as criticizing you in any way, Edith?"

"Not at all—"

She paused. Bartholomew had uttered a grunt. She turned and saw that he had left his desk and was standing at the window.

"What is it?" demanded Henry.

"People," said Bartholomew, and then after an instant: "Whole jam of them. They're coming from Sixth Avenue."

"People?"

The fat man pressed his nose to the pane.

"Soldiers, by God!" he said emphatically. "I had an idea they'd come back."

Edith jumped to her feet, and running over joined Bartholomew at the window.

"There's a lot of them!" she cried excitedly. "Come here, Henry!"

Henry readjusted his shade, but kept his seat.

"Hadn't we better turn out the lights?" suggested Bartholomew.

"No. They'll go away in a minute."

"They're not," said Edith, peering from the window. "They're not even thinking of going away. There's more of them coming. Look—there's a whole crowd turning the corner of Sixth Avenue."

By the yellow glow and blue shadows of the street lamp she could see that the sidewalk was crowded with men. They were mostly in uniform, some sober, some enthusiastically drunk, and over the whole swept an incoherent clamor and shouting.

Henry rose, and going to the window exposed himself as a long silhouette against the office lights. Immediately the shouting became a steady yell, and a rattling fusillade of small missiles, corners of tobacco plugs, cigarette boxes, and even pennies beat against the window. The sounds of the racket now began floating up the stairs as the folding doors revolved.

"They're coming up!" cried Bartholomew.

Edith turned anxiously to Henry.

"They're coming up, Henry."

From downstairs in the lower hall their cries were now quite audible.

"—God damn Socialists!"

"Pro-Germans! Boche-lovers!"

"Second floor, front! Come on!"

"We'll get the sons—"

The next five minutes passed in a dream. Edith was conscious that the clamor burst suddenly upon the three of them like a cloud of rain, that there was a thunder of many feet on the stairs, that Henry had seized her arm and drawn her back toward the rear of the office. Then the door opened and an overflow of men were forced into the room—not the leaders, but simply those who happened to be in front.

"Hello, Bo!"

"Up late, ain't you?"

"You an' your girl. Damn *you*!"

She noticed that two very drunken soldiers had been forced to the front, where they wobbled fatuously—one of them was short and dark, the other was tall and weak of chin.

Henry stepped forward and raised his hand.

"Friends!" he said.

The clamor faded into a momentary stillness, punctuated with mutterings.

"Friends!" he repeated, his far-away eyes fixed over the heads of the crowd, "you're injuring no one but yourselves by breaking in here tonight. Do we look like rich men? Do we look like Germans? I ask you in all fairness—"

"Pipe down!"

"I'll say you do!"

"Say, who's your lady friend, buddy?"

A man in civilian clothes, who had been pawing over a table, suddenly held up a newspaper.

"Here it is!" he shouted. "They wanted the Germans to win the war!"

A new overflow from the stairs was shouldered in and of a sudden the room was full of men all closing around the pale little group at the back. Edith saw that the tall soldier with the weak chin was still in front. The short dark one had disappeared.

She edged slightly backward, stood close to the open window, through which came a clear breath of cool night air.

Then the room was a riot. She realized that the soldiers were surging forward, glimpsed the fat man swinging a chair over his head—instantly the lights went out, and she felt the push of warm bodies under rough cloth, and her ears were full of shouting and trampling and hard breathing.

A figure flashed by her out of nowhere, tottered, was edged sideways, and of a sudden disappeared helplessly out through the open window with a frightened, fragmentary cry that died staccato on the bosom of the clamor. By the faint light streaming from the building backing on the area Edith had a quick impression that it had been the tall soldier with the weak chin.

Anger rose astonishingly in her. She swung her arms wildly, edged blindly toward the thickest of the scuffling. She heard grunts, curses, the muffled impact of fists.

"Henry!" she called frantically, "Henry!"

Then, it was minutes later, she felt suddenly that there were other figures in the room. She heard a voice, deep, bullying, authoritative; she saw yellow rays of light sweeping here and there in the fracas. The cries became more scattered. The scuffling increased and then stopped.

Suddenly the lights were on and the room was full of policemen, clubbing left and right. The deep voice boomed out:

"Here now! Here now! Here now!"

And then:

"Quiet down and get out! Here now!"

The room seemed to empty like a washbowl. A policeman fast-grappled in the corner released his hold on his soldier antagonist and started him with a shove toward the door. The deep voice continued. Edith perceived now that it came from a bull-necked police captain standing near the door.

"Here now! This is no way! One of your own sojers got shoved out of the back window an' killed hisself!"

"Henry!" called Edith, "Henry!"

She beat wildly with her fists on the back of the man in front of her; she brushed between two others; fought, shrieked, and beat her way to a very pale figure sitting on the floor close to a desk.

"Henry," she cried passionately, "what's the matter? What's the matter? Did they hurt you?"

His eyes were shut. He groaned and then looking up said disgustedly—

"They broke my leg. My God, the fools!"

"Here now!" called the police captain. "Here now! Here now!"

IX

"Childs', Fifty-ninth Street," at eight o'clock of any morning differs from its sisters by less than the width of their marble tables or the degree of polish on the frying pans. You will see there a crowd of poor people with sleep in the corners of their eyes, trying to look straight before them at their food so as not to see the other poor people. But Childs', Fifty-ninth, four hours earlier is quite unlike any Childs' restaurant from Portland, Oregon, to Portland, Maine. Within its pale but sanitary walls one finds a noisy medley of chorus girls, college boys, debutantes, rakes, *filles de joie*—a not unrepresentative mixture of the gayest of Broadway, and even of Fifth Avenue.

In the early morning of May the second it was unusually full. Over the marble-topped tables were bent the excited faces of flappers whose fathers owned individual villages. They were eating buckwheat cakes and scrambled eggs with relish and gusto, an accomplishment that it would have been utterly impossible for them to repeat in the same place four hours later.

Almost the entire crowd were from the Gamma Psi dance at Delmonico's except for several chorus girls from a midnight revue who sat at a side table and wished they'd taken off a little more make-up after the show. Here and there a drab, mouse-like figure, desperately out of place, watched the butterflies with a weary, puzzled curiosity. But the drab figure was the exception. This was the morning after May Day, and celebration was still in the air.

Gus Rose, sober but a little dazed, must be classed as one of the drab figures. How he had got himself from Forty-fourth Street to Fifty-ninth Street after the riot was only a hazy half-memory. He had seen the body of Carrol Key put in an ambulance and driven off, and then he had started up town with two or three soldiers. Somewhere between Forty-fourth Street and Fifty-ninth Street the other soldiers had met some women and disappeared. Rose had wandered to Columbus Circle and chosen the gleaming lights of Childs' to minister to his craving for coffee and doughnuts. He walked in and sat down.

All around him floated airy, inconsequential chatter and high-pitched laughter. At first he failed to understand, but after a puzzled five minutes he realized that this was the aftermath of some gay party. Here and there a restless, hilarious young man wandered fraternally and familiarly between the tables, shaking hands indiscriminately and pausing occasionally for a facetious chat, while excited waiters, bearing cakes and eggs aloft, swore at him silently, and bumped him out of the way. To Rose, seated at the most inconspicuous and least crowded table, the whole scene was a colorful circus of beauty and riotous pleasure.

He became gradually aware, after a few moments, that the couple seated diagonally across from him, with their backs to the crowd, were not the least interesting pair in the room. The man was drunk. He wore a dinner coat with a dishevelled tie and shirt swollen by spillings of water and wine. His eyes, dim and bloodshot, roved unnaturally from side to side. His breath came short between his lips.

"He's been on a spree!" thought Rose.

The woman was almost if not quite sober. She was pretty, with dark eyes and feverish high color, and she kept her active eyes fixed on her companion with the alertness of a hawk. From time to time she would lean and whisper intently to him, and he would answer by inclining his head heavily or by a particularly ghoulish and repellent wink.

Rose scrutinized them dumbly for some minutes, until the woman gave him a quick, resentful look; then he shifted his gaze to two of the most conspicuously hilarious of the promenaders who were on a protracted circuit of the tables. To his surprise he recognized in one of them the young man by whom he had been so ludicrously entertained at Delmonico's. This started him thinking of Key with a vague sentimentality, not unmixed with awe. Key was dead. He had fallen thirty-five feet and split his skull like a cracked cocoanut.

"He was a darn good guy," thought Rose mournfully. "He was a darn good guy, o'right. That was awful hard luck about him."

The two promenaders approached and started down between Rose's table and the next, addressing friends and strangers alike with jovial familiarity. Suddenly Rose saw the fair-haired one with the prominent teeth stop, look unsteadily at the man and girl opposite, and then begin to move his head disapprovingly from side to side.

The man with the bloodshot eyes looked up.

"Gordy," said the promenader with the prominent teeth, "Gordy."

"Hello," said the man with the stained shirt thickly.

Prominent Teeth shook his finger pessimistically at the pair, giving the woman a glance of aloof condemnation.

"What'd I tell you Gordy?"

Gordon stirred in his seat.

"Go to hell!" he said.

Dean continued to stand there shaking his finger. The woman began to get angry.

"You go way!" she cried fiercely. "You're drunk, that's what you are!"

"So's he," suggested Dean, staying the motion of his finger and pointing it at Gordon.

Peter Himmel ambled up, owlish now and oratorically inclined.

"Here now," he began as if called upon to deal with some petty dispute between children. "Wha's all trouble?"

"You take your friend away," said Jewel tartly. "He's bothering us."

"What's 'at?"

"You heard me!" she said shrilly. "I said to take your drunken friend away."

Her rising voice rang out above the clatter of the restaurant and a waiter came hurrying up.

"You gotta be more quiet!"

"That fella's drunk," she cried. "He's insulting us."

"Ah-ha, Gordy," persisted the accused. "What'd I tell you." He turned to the waiter. "Gordy an' I friends. Been tryin' help him, haven't I, Gordy?"

Gordy looked up.

"Help me? Hell, no!"

Jewel rose suddenly, and seizing Gordon's arm assisted him to his feet.

"Come on, Gordy!" she said, leaning toward him and speaking in a half whisper. "Let's us get out of here. This fella's got a mean drunk on."

Gordon allowed himself to be urged to his feet

and started toward the door. Jewel turned for a second and addressed the provoker of their flight.

"I know all about *you!*" she said fiercely. "Nice friend, you are, I'll say. He told me about you."

Then she seized Gordon's arm, and together they made their way through the curious crowd, paid their check, and went out.

"You'll have to sit down," said the waiter to Peter after they had gone.

"What's 'at? Sit down?"

"Yes—or get out."

Peter turned to Dean.

"Come on," he suggested. "Let's beat up this waiter."

"All right."

They advanced toward him, their faces grown stern. The waiter retreated.

Peter suddenly reached over to a plate on the table beside him and picking up a handful of hash tossed it into the air. It descended as a languid parabola in snowflake effect on the heads of those near by.

"Hey! Ease up!"

"Put him out!"

"Sit down, Peter!"

"Cut out that stuff!"

Peter laughed and bowed.

"Thank you for your kind applause, ladies and gents. If some one will lend me some more hash and a tall hat we will go on with the act."

The bouncer bustled up.

"You've gotta get out!" he said to Peter.

"Hell, no!"

"He's my friend!" put in Dean indignantly.

A crowd of waiters were gathering. "Put him out!"

"Better go, Peter."

There was a short struggle and the two were edged and pushed toward the door.

"I got a hat and a coat here!" cried Peter.

"Well, go get 'em and be spry about it!"

The bouncer released his hold on Peter, who, adopting a ludicrous air of extreme cunning, rushed immediately around to the other table, where he burst into derisive laughter and thumbed his nose at the exasperated waiters.

"Think I just better wait a l'il' longer," he announced.

The chase began. Four waiters were sent around one way and four another. Dean caught hold of two of them by the coat, and another struggle took place before the pursuit of Peter could be resumed; he was finally pinioned after overturning a sugar-bowl and several cups of coffee. A fresh argument ensued at the cashier's desk, where Peter attempted to buy another dish of hash to take with him and throw at policemen.

But the commotion upon his exit proper was dwarfed by another phenomenon which drew admiring glances and a prolonged involuntary "Oh-h-h!" from every person in the restaurant.

The great plate-glass front had turned to a deep creamy blue, the color of a Maxfield Parrish moonlight— a blue that seemed to press close upon the pane as if to crowd its way into the restaurant. Dawn had come up in Columbus Circle, magical, breathless dawn, silhouetting the great statue of the immortal Christopher, and mingling in a curious and uncanny manner with the fading yellow electric light inside.

X   Mr. In and Mr. Out are not listed by the census-taker. You will search for them in vain through the social register or the births, marriages, and deaths, or the grocer's credit list. Oblivion has swallowed them and the testimony that they ever existed at all is vague and shadowy, and inadmissible in a court of law. Yet I have it upon the best authority that for a brief space Mr. In and Mr. Out lived, breathed, answered to their names and radiated vivid personalities of their own.

During the brief span of their lives they walked in their native garments down the great highway of a great nation; were laughed at, sworn at, chased, and fled from. Then they passed and were heard of no more.

They were already taking form dimly, when a taxicab with the top open breezed down Broadway in the faintest glimmer of May dawn. In this car sat the souls of Mr. In and Mr. Out discussing with amazement the blue light that had so precipitately colored the sky behind the statue of Christopher Columbus, discussing with bewilderment the old, gray faces of the early risers which skimmed palely along the street like blown bits of paper on a gray lake. They were agreed on all things, from the absurdity of the bouncer in Childs' to the absurdity of the business of life. They were dizzy with the extreme maudlin happiness that the morning had awakened in their glowing souls. Indeed, so fresh and vigorous was their pleasure in living that they felt it should be expressed by loud cries.

"Ye-ow-ow!" hooted Peter, making a megaphone with his hands—and Dean joined in with a call that, though equally significant and symbolic, derived its resonance from its very inarticulateness.

"Yo-ho! Yea! Yoho! Yo-buba!"

Fifty-third Street was a bus with a dark, bobbed-hair beauty atop; Fifty-second was a street cleaner who dodged, escaped, and sent up a yell of "Look where you're aimin'!" in a pained and grieved voice. At Fiftieth Street a group of men on a very white sidewalk in front of a very white building turned to stare after them, and shouted:

"Some party, boys!"

At Forty-ninth Street Peter turned to Dean. "Beautiful morning," he said gravely, squinting up his owlish eyes.

"Probably is."

"Go get some breakfast, hey?"

Dean agreed—with additions.

"Breakfast and liquor."

"Breakfast and liquor," repeated Peter, and they looked at each other, nodding. "That's logical."

Then they both burst into loud laughter.

"Breakfast and liquor! Oh, gosh!"

"No such thing," announced Peter.

"Don't serve it? Ne'mind. We force 'em serve it. Bring pressure bear."

"Bring logic bear."

The taxi cut suddenly off Broadway, sailed along a cross street, and stopped in front of a heavy tomblike building in Fifth Avenue.

"What's idea?"

The taxi driver informed them that this was Delmonico's.

This was somewhat puzzling. They were forced to devote several minutes to intense concentration, for if such an order had been given there must have been a reason for it.

"Somep'm 'bout a coat," suggested the taxi-man.

That was it. Peter's overcoat and hat. He had left them at Delmonico's. Having decided this, they disembarked from the taxi and strolled toward the entrance arm in arm.

"Hey!" said the taxi driver.

"Huh?"

"You better pay me."

They shook their heads in shocked negation.

"Later, not now—we give orders, you wait."

The taxi driver objected; he wanted his money now. With the scornful condescension of men exercising tremendous self-control they paid him.

Inside Peter groped in vain through a dim, deserted check-room in search of his coat and derby.

"Gone, I guess. Somebody stole it."

"Some Sheff student."

"All probability."

"Never mind," said Dean, nobly. "I'll leave mine here too—then we'll both be dressed the same."

He removed his overcoat and hat and was hanging them up when his roving glance was caught and held magnetically by two large squares of cardboard tacked to the two coatroom doors. The one on the left-hand door bore the word "In" in big black letters, and the one on the right-hand door flaunted the equally emphatic word "Out."

"Look!" he exclaimed happily——

Peter's eyes followed his pointing finger.

"What?"

"Look at the signs. Let's take 'em."

"Good idea."

"Probably pair very rare an' valuable signs. Probably come in handy."

Peter removed the left-hand sign from the door and endeavored to conceal it about his person. The sign being of considerable proportions, this was a matter of some difficulty. An idea flung itself at him, and with an air of dignified mystery he turned his back. After an instant he wheeled dramatically around, and stretching out his arms displayed himself to the admiring Dean. He had inserted the sign in his vest, completely covering his shirt front. In effect, the word "In" had been painted upon his shirt in large black letters.

"Yoho!" cheered Dean. "Mister In."

He inserted his own sign in like manner.

"Mister Out!" he announced triumphantly. "Mr. In meet Mr. Out."

They advanced and shook hands. Again laughter overcame them and they rocked in a shaken spasm of mirth.

"Yoho!"

"We probably get a flock of breakfast."

"We'll go—go to the Commodore."

Arm in arm they sallied out the door, and turning east on Forty-fourth Street set out for the Commodore.

As they came out a short dark soldier, very pale and tired, who had been wandering listlessly along the sidewalk, turned to look at them.

He started over as though to address them, but as they immediately bent on him glances of withering unrecognition, he waited until they had started unsteadily down the street, and then followed at about forty paces, chuckling to himself and saying "Oh, boy!" over and over under his breath, in delighted, anticipatory tones.

Mr. In and Mr. Out were meanwhile exchanging pleasantries concerning their future plans.

"We want liquor; we want breakfast. Neither without the other. One and indivisible."

"We want both 'em!"

"Both 'em!"

It was quite light now, and passers-by began to bend curious eyes on the pair. Obviously they were engaged in a discussion, which afford each of them intense amusement, for occasionally a fit of laughter would seize upon them so violently that, still with their arms interlocked, they would bend nearly double.

Reaching the Commodore, they exchanged a few spicy epigrams with the sleepy-eyed doorman, navigated the revolving door with some difficulty, and then made their way through a thinly populated but startled lobby to the dining room, where a puzzled waiter showed them an obscure table in a corner. They studied the bill of fare helplessly, telling over the items to each other in puzzled mumbles.

"Don't see any liquor here," said Peter reproachfully.

The waiter became audible but unintelligible.

"Repeat," continued Peter, with patient tolerance, "that there seems to be unexplained and quite distasteful lack of liquor upon bill of fare."

"Here!" said Dean confidently, "let me handle him." He turned to the waiter—"Bring us—bring us—" he scanned the bill of fare anxiously. "Bring us a quart of champagne and a—a—probably ham sandwich."

The waiter looked doubtful.

"Bring it!" roared Mr. In and Mr. Out in chorus.

The waiter coughed and disappeared. There was a short wait during which they were subjected without their knowledge to a careful scrutiny by the headwaiter. Then the champagne arrived, and at the sight of it Mr. In and Mr. Out became jubilant.

"Imagine their objecting to us having champagne for breakfast—jus' imagine."

They both concentrated upon the vision of such an awesome possibility, but the feat was too much for them. It was impossible for their joint imaginations to conjure up a world where any one might object to any one else having champagne for breakfast. The waiter drew the cork with an enormous *pop*—and their glasses immediately foamed with pale yellow froth.

"Here's health, Mr. In."

"Here's same to you, Mr. Out."

The waiter withdrew; the minutes passed; the champagne became low in the bottle.

"It's—it's mortifying," said Dean suddenly.

"Wha's mortifying?"

"The idea their objecting us having champagne breakfast."

"Mortifying?" Peter considered. "Yes, tha's word—mortifying."

Again they collapsed into laughter, howled, swayed, rocked back and forth in their chairs, repeating the word "mortifying" over and over to each other—each repetition seeming to make it only more brilliantly absurd.

After a few more gorgeous minutes they decided on another quart. Their anxious waiter consulted his immediate superior, and this discreet person gave implicit instructions that no more champagne should be served. Their check was brought.

Five minutes later, arm in arm, they left the Commodore and made their way through a curious, staring crowd along Forty-second Street, and up Vanderbilt Avenue to the Biltmore. There, with sudden cunning, they rose to the occasion and traversed the lobby, walking fast and standing unnaturally erect.

Once in the dining room they repeated their performance. They were torn between intermittent convulsive laughter and sudden spasmodic discussions of politics, college, and the sunny state of their dispositions. Their watches told them that it was now nine o'clock, and a dim idea was born in them that they were on a memorable party, something that they would remember always. They lingered over the second bottle. Either of them had only to mention the word "mortifying" to send them both into riotous gasps. The dining room was whirring and shifting now; a curious lightness permeated and rarefied the heavy air.

They paid their check and walked out into the lobby.

It was at this moment that the exterior doors revolved for the thousandth time that morning, and admitted into the lobby a very pale young beauty with dark circles under her eyes, attired in a much-rumpled evening dress. She was accompanied by a plain stout man, obviously not an appropriate escort.

At the top of the stairs this couple encountered Mr. In and Mr. Out.

"Edith," began Mr. In, stepping toward her hilariously and making a sweeping bow, "darling, good morning."

The stout man glanced questioningly at Edith, as if merely asking her permission to throw this man summarily out of the way.

"'Scuse familiarity," added Peter, as an afterthought. "Edith, good morning."

He seized Dean's elbow and impelled him into the foreground.

"Meet Mr. In, Edith, my bes' frien'. Inseparable. Mr. In and Mr. Out."

Mr. Out advanced and bowed; in fact, he advanced so far and bowed so low that he tipped slightly forward and only kept his balance by placing a hand lightly on Edith's shoulder.

"I'm Mr. Out, Edith," he mumbled pleasantly, "S'misterin Misterout."

"'Smisterinanout," said Peter proudly.

But Edith stared straight by them, her eyes fixed on some infinite speck in the gallery above her. She nodded slightly to the stout man, who advanced bull-like and with a sturdy brisk gesture pushed Mr. In and Mr. Out to either side. Through this alley he and Edith walked.

But ten paces farther on Edith stopped again—

stopped and pointed to a short, dark soldier who was eying the crowd in general, and the tableau of Mr. In and Mr. Out in particular, with a sort of puzzled, spellbound awe.

"There," cried Edith. "See there!"

Her voice rose, became somewhat shrill. Her pointing finger shook slightly.

"There's the soldier who broke my brother's leg."

There were a dozen exclamations; a man in a cutaway coat left his place near the desk and advanced alertly; the stout person made a sort of lightning-like spring toward the short, dark soldier, and then the lobby closed around the little group and blotted them from the sight of Mr. In and Mr. Out.

But to Mr. In and Mr. Out this event was merely a parti-colored iridescent segment of a whirring, spinning world.

They heard loud voices; they saw the stout man spring; the picture suddenly blurred.

Then they were in an elevator bound skyward.

"What floor, please?" said the elevator man.

"Any floor," said Mr. In.

"Top floor," said Mr. Out.

"This is the top floor," said the elevator man.

"Have another floor put on," said Mr. Out.

"Higher," said Mr. In.

"Heaven," said Mr. Out.

In a bedroom of a small hotel just off Sixth Avenue Gordon Sterrett awoke with a pain in the back of his head and a sick throbbing in all his veins. He looked at the dusky gray shadows in the corners of the room and at a raw place on a large leather chair in the corner where it had long been in use. He saw clothes, disheveled, rumpled clothes on the floor and he smelt stale cigarette smoke and stale liquor. The windows were tight shut. Outside the bright sunlight had thrown a dust-filled beam across the sill—a beam broken by the head of the wide wooden bed in which he had slept. He lay very quiet— comatose, drugged, his eyes wide, his mind clicking wildly like an unoiled machine.

It must have been thirty seconds after he perceived the sunbeam with the dust on it and the rip on the large leather chair that he had the sense of life close beside him, and it was another thirty seconds after that before he realized that he was irrevocably married to Jewel Hudson.

He went out half an hour later and bought a revolver at a sporting goods store. Then he took a taxi to the room where he had been living on East Twenty-seventh Street, and, leaning across the table that held his drawing materials, fired a cartridge into his head just behind the temple.

OTHER TITLES IN
THE ART OF THE NOVELLA SERIES

BARTLEBY THE SCRIVENER / HERMAN MELVILLE
THE LESSON OF THE MASTER / HENRY JAMES
MY LIFE / ANTON CHEKHOV
THE DEVIL / LEO TOLSTOY
THE TOUCHSTONE / EDITH WHARTON
THE HOUND OF THE BASKERVILLES / ARTHUR CONAN DOYLE
THE DEAD / JAMES JOYCE
FIRST LOVE / IVAN TURGENEV
A SIMPLE HEART / GUSTAVE FLAUBERT
THE MAN WHO WOULD BE KING / RUDYARD KIPLING
MICHAEL KOHLHAAS / HEINRICH VON KLEIST
THE BEACH OF FALESÁ / ROBERT LOUIS STEVENSON
THE HORLA / GUY DE MAUPASSANT
THE ETERNAL HUSBAND / FYODOR DOSTOEVSKY
THE MAN THAT CORRUPTED HADLEYBURG / MARK TWAIN
THE LIFTED VEIL / GEORGE ELIOT
THE GIRL WITH THE GOLDEN EYES / HONORÉ DE BALZAC
A SLEEP AND A FORGETTING / WILLIAM DEAN HOWELLS
BENITO CERENO / HERMAN MELVILLE
MATHILDA / MARY SHELLEY
STEMPENYU: A JEWISH ROMANCE / SHOLEM ALEICHEM
FREYA OF THE SEVEN ISLES / JOSEPH CONRAD
HOW THE TWO IVANS QUARRELLED / NIKOLAI GOGOL
MAY DAY / F. SCOTT FITZGERALD
RASSELAS, PRINCE ABYSSINIA / SAMUEL JOHNSON
THE DIALOGUE OF THE DOGS / MIGUEL DE CERVANTES
THE LEMOINE AFFAIR / MARCEL PROUST
THE COXON FUND / HENRY JAMES
THE DEATH OF IVAN ILYICH / LEO TOLSTOY
TALES OF BELKIN / ALEXANDER PUSHKIN

30 July. 11

Amazon 8-0

114/60